Loving You

Xpress Yourself Publishing

Loving You

A Novella

JESSICA TILLES

To love...one day, you'll find me again.

OTHER TITLES BY JESSICA TILLES

Anything Goes

In My Sisters' Corner

Sweet Revenge

Fatal Desire

Unfinished Business

Apple Tree

Erogenous Zone (Anthology)

Loving Simone

Crossing Sisters

No One Has To Know (with William Fredrick Cooper)

The Triumph of My Soul (anthology, contributor)

ACKNOWLEDGMENTS

Serenity is peace amid the storm.

God, I am nothing without You.

Mama and Daddy: I wish you were here.

Teddy, my beautiful, furbaby: I miss you deeply.

Steven E. LaBroi: Thank you...for everything. Seriously!

Bill Holmes: You make this literary road less bumpy.

Friends, family, and extended family: Thank you for your continued love and support.

To the fantastic, phenomenal, and amazing book clubs that have supported me throughout my eighteen-year literary journey, beginning with *Anything Goes*—THANK YOU!

A warm, special thank you to the Jackson Mississippi Readers Club. I will get back to the 'Sip one day.

Ella Curry: Your friendship means the world to me.

Jo "Josie" Meeks: I love you, sister. 'Nough said. Thanks for proofreading *Loving You*. You're such the commaholic.

Believe there are no limits but the sky and you will soar high!

With love,
Jessica Tilles
September 1, 2018
9:25 p.m.

Lovin' you is easy 'cause you're beautiful
Makin' love with you is all I wanna do
Lovin' you is more than just a dream come true
And everything that I do is out of lovin' you

— "Lovin' You" by Minnie Ripperton

Chapter 1

The loud, beeping alarm clock jarred Julian Winters out of a peaceful slumber, as he smacked the off button. Waking up was no longer a pleasure. Rolling over onto his back, he blinked, closed his eyes, and then blinked again. Streaks of sunlight penetrated the window, blinding him. He rose up, dragged his feet off the bed, and rubbed the sleep from his eyes with his knuckles. He stretched his arms above his head, arched his back, and yawned. He looked over his shoulder, closed his eyes, and inhaled. He could still smell Moonlight Path, her favorite Bath & Body Works fragrance. He missed her so, as he rested his elbows on his knees and cradled his head in his hands. His throat tightened, nostrils burned, and eyes welled, a feeling to which he had become accustomed. Squeezing his head, he raised it as his fingertips dragged down his face, caressing his chin. He rolled his eyes upward.

I don't understand why any of this is happening, Julian thought, massaging the tension from the back of his neck. He remembered the words his mother spoke to him as a young boy whenever he was overwhelmed by impatience. "Not everything is meant for you to understand, son. When God is ready to tell you, He will. You must have patience."

"I guess He's not ready and I'm running out of patience," he mumbled.

Julian stood and arched his back. With his hands on his hips, he stretched from side to side, a ritual he performed every morning. He padded his bare feet across the room, into the master bathroom, and into the water closet. He didn't close the door to the room that contained a single flush toilet before aiming for the commode, but she was not there to gripe. He missed that, too. He turned on the shower. As he pulled his T-shirt over his head, the landline rang. In a swift motion, he dropped the shirt to the floor and rushed into the bedroom, rounding the bed to the nightstand to answer the phone.

"Yeah, hello," he answered, winded, with his hand propped on his hip, his head bowed.

"Hi, honey!"

Smiling, Julian sat on the edge of the bed. Even though it wasn't the voice he wanted to hear, it warmed his heart all the same.

"Hey, Mom. How are you?"

"I'm good, honey."

"And, Dad, how's he doing?"

"Your father is doing fine. He sends his love."

Constant deep sighs from his mother assured him he needed to get comfortable. Julian crossed his legs at the ankles, relaxed his posture, and settled in for what would come next.

"What's wrong, Mom?"

"Your father and I worry about you."

"I'm good, Mom."

"Are you sure? I'm your mother. I'm going to worry about you. Are you eating?"

"Yes, I'm eating." He lay back on the bed, stretching his free arm above his head.

"Well…" She sighed. "Well…"

Focusing on the cobwebs in the corner of the ceiling, he realized he needed to call a cleaning company. Housecleaning was not his thing.

As he listened to his mother hem and haw, struggling to find the right words, he simply said, "She's fine."

"Well," she said, sounding relieved. "You know, your father and I were planning to visit, but you know he has that big conference going on this week."

"It's okay, Mom. She'll understand."

"Okay. Well, honey, I won't hold you. I love you, son."

"Love you, too, Mom."

"We love Gracie so much."

"She knows."

Soft whimpers left her lips to his ears. "Oh, Julian!"

He closed his eyes and allowed her to have her moment as she wept.

"Honey?"

"Yeah."

"Please give her our love." Her voice cracked. "I want her to know how much—"

"I will, Mom. I'll call you later."

Behind a soft sniffle, she ended with, "Bye, honey."

After showering and dressing in blue Nike training shorts and matching hoodie, Julian headed for the kitchen, Grace's favorite room in the house. It was empty, devoid of sound, only emitting the smell of fresh coffee that had brewed in the automatic coffee maker an hour before he rose. He looked at the coffee pot and smiled. "Black coffee, no sugar, no cream, just like my man," she would always say in a singsong fashion each time he poured her a cup of coffee.

Julian moved toward the refrigerator, opened the freezer, and glared at the many frozen meals she had prepared before her long hospital stay. *Did she know,* he wondered, *that she wouldn't be returning?* An emotion lodged in his throat. He swallowed hard and closed the freezer door. He wasn't hungry anyway. His hearty appetite left when she left.

He shoved his hands in the pockets of the hoodie and stared at the sunflower wallpaper. Julian hated it when she chose it, but pretended to love it when she purchased it. *It is still ugly*, he thought, remembering the day she talked him into hanging it.

"The kitchen should be bright and full of life." That was her reason for choosing ugly wallpaper.

"True, but sunflowers? I feel like I'm in a field."

"Julian, don't be silly. The wallpaper is beautiful, just like you."

Julian blushed at his recollection. She always hurled the sweetest words from her arsenal of loving compliments. He never recalled a negative word ever slipping from her lips, even in the midst of anger. Fact is, they didn't argue. It wasn't in her nature, and he adored her too much to speak harsh words to her.

Grabbing an apple from the fruit bowl sitting on top of the kitchen island, Julian headed toward the garage door. As he wrapped his lips around it to take a bite, an eerie feeling enveloped him. Chills caressed his spine. With his feet planted to the floor, he was unable to move. He stood still for a few moments before he took a step backward and faced the golden-rod colored telephone hanging on the wall. Circa 1970, the telephone belonged to Grace's grandmother. Several years ago when her grandmother died, that old phone was something she just had to have. He shivered. There it was again, that feeling of emptiness and loss, knotting in his stomach.

Julian rushed toward the phone and picked up the receiver. With his index finger, he punched each key with intensity. He did not need to pull out his cell phone to retrieve the phone number. He had memorized it the day he left her at the hospital.

"Thank you for calling Holy Cross. How may I direct your call?"

"Room 303H, please." His request was loud and urgent.

"Sure. Have a great day." Her perky demeanor irritated him, causing the escape of a long sigh.

Julian's heart pounded with each ring. "Please pick up, baby." With closed eyes, *Oh, God, not now*, he prayed, and on the third ring, he slammed his palm against the wall, thinking the worst. "Damn—"

"Hello." Her tiny, weak voice slowed his racing heart.

He relaxed his posture and leaned against the wall. "Babe?"

With as much strength as she could muster, Grace sat up in the bed and moved the phone's receiver to her other ear.

"Hi, honey. Are you okay?" She knew something was wrong. She could hear it in his voice. "What's wrong, Julian?"

"Nothing." He hung his head low and mouthed, *Thank you, God.* He was listening after all.

"Then why aren't you smiling?"

"Huh?"

"You sound like you're frowning."

He chuckled and forced a smile just for her. It always amazed him that she knew him so well. "Is this better?"

She smiled, too. "Much. Now, what's going on?"

"Nothing. I just wanted to hear your voice. How did you sleep?"

Grace grunted. "It's hard to sleep in this place. Folks coming in every hour on the hour, checking this, that, and the other."

"It is for your own good."

She grunted, again. "So they tell me." Grace looked around the room, wishing she were home, anywhere except in a cold, sterilized hospital room. "Are you coming today?"

Julian rested his head against the sunflower wallpaper. "I come every day, Gracie."

She chuckled. "No, you don't."

"What?"

"You don't come *in me* every day." She let out soft, weak laughter, followed by a subtle cough.

He smirked. "You don't know how much I want to, babe."

Grace reclined her head against the pillow. "Don't I wish; the last time you were inside me… Wait, I can't even remember!"

"We've been through this—"

"Yes, I know, you don't want to hurt me. Got it. When are you coming?"

"After my run."

"Okay, honey. I'll see you when you get here."

"Do you need anything?"

"Just you and your hot rod." She smiled and hung up the phone before he could reply.

He chuckled. Hearing her voice was exactly what he needed. Feeling relieved, Julian picked up his keys off the island and exited through the door leading into the garage. He came upon the red Fiat® 124 Spider Classica convertible. It was hers. He had given it to her…just because.

After giving a soft tap to the garage opener, which hung on the wall, the door raised. It was an autumn day. Far enough from summer to have lost the scorching heat, but not close enough to winter for the blistering cold. The leaves had begun to fall and rain was in the forecast. The air was as crisp and sweet as the apple lodged in his mouth. He zipped up his hoodie and headed out for his daily run.

After a few stretches, Julian hit the sidewalk and began to jog. He never ran. His slow gait was almost soundless as his running shoes tapped the concrete, with hopes that the exercise would clear his mind.

Chapter 2

For an hour, Julian peered through the blinds that covered the bay window in Grace's hospital room. He wished he were amongst the traffic barreling up and down Interstate 495. He would give anything to escape the horrid smell that turned his stomach every time he stepped foot inside any hospital. He hated it; hated being around sickness and death, and oftentimes he wanted to vomit, but he had no choice but to be there. For six months, it had been his home away from home.

Wrapping the drawstring around his hand into a fist, he gently raised the blinds, careful not to awaken her, pressed his palm against the cool windowpane, lowered his head, and stared down at the parking lot below. Drawing in a deep breath, Julian tried to suppress the inner pain, but found it difficult. He wanted to take her away to a destination where cancer did not run rampant, but he knew it was impossible and the inevitable was lurking around the corner as it had been for quite some time now. A tear straddled the rim of his eye, threatening to fall as it did every time he reminisced about the knot that lodged in his throat on the day they received the news five years earlier. He could still feel it as if it never left. That knot. *Fuck,* he cursed, as he rolled his neck around, stretching it from side to side.

Five years earlier...

It was one of the coldest days of winter, and a foot of glistening snow blanketed Prince George's County, Maryland. They had plans for dinner at her favorite restaurant, Ruth Chris, but they never made it.

As Grace lay across the bed, Julian entered the bedroom. "Our reservations are for eight, babe. I want to get an early start. You know the roads are fucked up."

"Can't we stay home tonight?"

"Why? I thought you were looking forward to it."

She rolled over onto her back and raised her legs in the air. "I was until..."

Shaking his head, he folded his arms over his chest and smiled. "Until..."

She lowered her legs and sat up on the bed. "It's cold and nasty out there. Besides, the roads are probably a mess, so why don't we stay home, light a few candles, pop the cork on a bottle of wine, and enjoy some *"us"* time? What do you say?"

His eyes smiled at her. "I say the roads are too much of a mess."

"Great!" She hopped off the bed, stood in the middle of the floor and peeled off her clothes, slowly swaying her hips, displaying her best stripper moves, as she hummed her version of a stripper's theme song.

Julian loved her games. With his hands propped on his hips, he leaned back against the wall, legs crossed at the ankles. The smile on his face coincided with his thoughts. He was planning to blow her back out if she kept it up.

Naked, Grace slightly turned, looked over her shoulder, and stroked her tongue across her bottom lip. She raised her arms above her head, clasped her hands, arched her back, and jiggled her ass, popping, dropping low, bending her ass over, and aiming her sweet cheeks in his direction.

Her foreplay driving him wild, Julian grabbed his crotch, and gently bit down on his bottom lip. *This woman here.*

Grace looked over her shoulder at him, licked her finger, and inserted it inside her wetness.

Damn it! She loves messing with me.

Two claps of his hands activated the stereo system and Stevie Wonder belted, "As around the sun the earth knows she's revolving," from his song "As," from the *Songs in the Key of Life* album. It was her favorite song.

Julian moved toward her and ran his hands over her round earth, sending electricity she needed to jump-start her engine. Bending down, his soft lips connected with her warm flesh, passionately kissing skin, from the crease to the arch of her back as Stevie Wonder sang words that sounded as if he had written them especially for Grace.

Standing, she faced him and kissed his lips. "Let's start in the shower."

Taking him by the hand, Grace walked into the master bathroom and sensually smacked her left cheek, arousing him even more.

She stepped inside the shower with him in tow. As she stood under the showerhead, Julian reached around her and turned it on. She cocked her head back, allowing water to rain down on her. He lathered the washcloth and washed her front, starting with her neck, down to her chest, across each breast, down to her stomach, stopping at her abdomen. He dropped the washcloth and moved in closer.

"Open your thighs," he said, barely above a whisper, only inches from her dripping wet lips.

Grace moved her feet, inches apart, with a slight squat, opening her thighs as it was now Eddie Levert's turn to belt out, "You Got The Hooks In Me."

Her lips parted. His tongue stroked her bottom lip. Their lips connected as he slid his finger up her slippery slope, slightly arching, and connecting with the small knot at the hood of her vagina.

It felt nice, and she moaned as their tongues danced. She caressed his manhood and stroked from the head to the shaft, teasing his testicles.

The urge to take her right there was too much. He broke their embrace and stepped back. Julian saw the scar that he'd seen so many times before, the size of a thumbtack, on her collarbone, the price she paid as a young girl playing in her uncle's barn in Emporia, Virginia, near exposed nails.

Holding her head back under the stream of warm water and closing her eyes tightly, Grace's mouth opened, releasing deep moans as he pinched each nipple and massaged each breast.

Suddenly, he stopped, dousing the flames ignited between them. When she raised her head and wiped her eyes, Grace saw a look of concern on his face. His hand still latched onto her left breast.

"What's wrong?"

Julian shook his head, unsure. *It's nothing,* he thought, but he couldn't shake that gut feeling.

He made eye contact with her. "Babe, I feel something."

"Huh?"

He took her hand and placed it over her left breast. "Right there." He guided her index finger over a tiny lump. "Do you feel it?"

She was quiet. She nodded.

Now noticing the sudden fear in her eyes, Julian said, "It may be nothing, but—"

"Yeah, it may be. I mean, you know there are tiny little lumps in the breasts anyway. I feel them all the time."

Grace tried to force a smile, but her gut instinct was telling her different.

"Yeah, I know, but…" he trailed off, trying to choose the right words. "Babe," he forced a smile, "I'm on your breast all the time. I know when I feel something different…something that's not right. This one is very hard. Those other tiny lumps you're referring to aren't hard and they are glands and feel like they belong." He sighed heavily. "This one doesn't feel that way. Babe, please…"

"I'll get it checked out."

She rinsed off and stepped out of the shower.

Julian watched her every move. He watched her dry off before wrapping the towel around her. As she was about to exit the bathroom, he called out to her.

Grace faced him. "I'm okay, honey."

"Are you sure?"

She smiled and nodded, but deep down inside she was petrified. Trying not to make any assumptions, she made a beeline for her cell phone and searched her list of contacts for her primary care physician. Grace placed the phone to her ear and stared out the window at their neighbor's children making angels in the snow while the parents shoveled the front walk. It was Sunday, so she knew she would have to leave a message. The long, drawn-out message was frustrating her. She always thought it was too damn long.

14

Thank you for calling the office of Doctor Jonathan Douglass. Our normal office hours are Monday through Friday, nine am to five pm, closed Saturday and Sunday. If this is an emergency, please hang up and dial 911. Please leave a message and we will return your call during normal business hours. Thank you!

The chipper recorded female voice did nothing to lift her spirits, just annoyed her because she would have to wait at least twenty-four hours to hear back from them.

"Hello. This is Grace Winters," she paused, taking a deep breath. "I have a lump in my breast. I would like to see Doctor Douglass as soon as possible, please. I can be reached at (301) 555-9645."

Three weeks, two mammograms, one sonogram, and one biopsy later, with bated breaths, Julian and Grace waited patiently in Exam Room 1 for Doctor Lockett, her oncologist.

"Everything is going to be fine," Grace reassured Julian, but his intuition told him otherwise. It never steered him wrong.

"What's taking him so long?" he huffed, a mixture of emotions building. If the doctor did not appear with answers soon, he was sure to explode.

"Honey, please try to relax. You are making me anxious." Grace squeezed his hand, extending him a smile that would forever warm his heart at the right moments.

He was calming. It was difficult for Julian to imagine living without that smile. The thought of possibly not having her around gnawed at his soul. Shaking his head, *I'm being silly*, he thought, so he chose to think positive thoughts. Grace was his angel, his ride or die, the protector of his heart, the lover of his soul. For her, he had to be strong.

A soft rap at the door had straightened both their postures.

"Come in," Grace said, stealing a quick glance at Julian. Fear racked her insides, too, causing her to shudder.

Anxiety masked her eyes. He squeezed her hand, lifted it to his lips, and kissed it. It calmed her, but not much.

Doctor Lockett entered the room with a solemn look. No smile. No raised brow. Nothing but a generic look which he held each time he had bad news to deliver. Devoid of emotions, say it quick, answer any questions, and leave the room. That was how he did it. Becoming emotionally involved with his patients was taboo. After all, he was only human. After twenty years of delivering bad news, he would have been committed to an asylum had he not followed his motto. Nor would he be able to provide appropriate, potentially life-saving care, if he operated based off his emotions.

"Don't beat around the fucking bush with me, Doctor Lockett!" Grace blurted before she realized she'd spoken, her tone harsh. She was not in the mood for hand-holding and prolonging the inevitable. She had researched her symptoms on the Internet. Like many others in the world of modern technology, she, too, had become a Google doctor. Grace knew; she just needed to hear the confirmation. "Do I have cancer or not?"

Julian peered at her with his mouth gaped open, surprised at her choice of words and the angst in her voice, but he understood. He gave her hand another squeeze, reassuring her.

"All right then..." Doctor Lockett sighed, sitting on the small, round stool, crossing his legs at the ankles. "It's not good."

"I have cancer?"

"Yes." He was straightforward with eye-to-eye contact. "Your treatment must be aggressive. I won't sugarcoat it, Mrs. Winters. You have a tough battle to fight."

"What stage?" she asked, now sitting erect, chin up, ready for battle.

"Stage Four."

Like a pin to a balloon, his words deflated her. Suddenly, she felt light-headed. She gripped Julian's hand and, as he stood, fell into his embrace.

Julian looked at Doctor Lockett with sadness in his eyes. "Are you absolutely sure?" He was hoping an error had taken place.

"Yes, Mr. Winters."

Grace managed to speak. "Julian, I'm going to die."

Her words were a knife to his heart. He, too, almost lost it. "No, you're not, Grace." He looked at Doctor Lockett for some kind of reassurance as he sat quietly on his stool. *Devoid of emotions, say it quick, answer any questions, and leave the room*, but he could not move fast enough.

Doctor Lockett sighed. "Mrs. Winters, many women survive Stage Four—"

"Take it. Take them both. I don't need them!" Grace barked out of fear.

"Honey, what are you talking about?"

She grabbed her breasts. "These. I can get new tits, ain't that right, Doctor?" She looked at Doctor Lockett. "Right? I can get me some J. Lo boobs!"

Doctor Lockett nodded. "If you wish."

"Honey, are you—" Julian started, but the look of desperation on his beloved's face caused him to recoil. "Well, J. Lo boobs it is."

Although Grace had a full mastectomy, followed by her J. Lo boobs, it had been a battle for them both for five years, six months, three days, and six hours. It had been a roller coaster ride of emotions, but they forged through without giving up. Twice, Grace's cancer had gone into remission, but this time was different. It returned and it wasn't leaving without her. She was losing her battle. She stopped fighting. She was tired.

As Julian raised his head, he peered out the window, gazing up at the blue sky, challenging his once strong faith in God. Daily, Julian questioned God, not knowing what He was trying to prove by taking away the most precious life that meant the world to him. Was it something he had done in his past that angered God? *That's it. It has to be it*, he thought. Julian had pissed off God, so He was taking his woman from him as his punishment. He knew God was a forgiving God, so why could He not forgive him of his past sins, whatever those were?

"Heavenly Father," he whispered. "I'd give my life for Gracie's. Please, God. Please, don't take her from me. Please, God, I beg your forgiveness for whatever I did. Sweet Jesus." His vision blinded by tears, an aching cry pained his chest.

Julian was not ready for her to go; he needed her here with him to live out the rest of their years together. They still had so much life to live. For God's sake, she was only forty-one and he was forty-four. Who was going to greet him every morning with grapefruit and hot tea in bed? Grace had spoiled him rotten, meeting all his needs. In return, though, he spoiled her, too, if not more.

Through fifteen years of marriage, each day brought on a different Grace: intriguing and full of life. She never failed to amaze him. It was her intent from the first day she laid eyes on Julian to keep the spice in their lives until death did them part. She planned to keep her word.

Chapter 3

Too feeble to toss and turn, Grace was having a good dream. It was receding and her intimate affair with Chiwetel Ejiofor was ending. Her nose twitched at the familiar masculine scent of Bleu De Chanel, forming her thin lips into a faint smile. It was her favorite, and Julian always wore it for her. Fortunately, awkward smells did not make her sick. She stretched her eyes open and looked around the room until they landed on him.

An exhausting sigh escaped her. "What are you doing, fussing again, honey?"

Although weak, her soothing angelic voice enveloped him like a thick, warm blanket on a cold Christmas morning. It felt warm and comforting. Everything about her felt good to him. Grace was the tonic that healed all his ailments. Now what would Julian do when he no longer had that healing? The idea of it all was like a sucker punch to his gut.

He smiled. Her voice has been sweet music to his ears, a melody of her own, never replicated or duplicated. Like the late Minnie Ripperton, she could sing, too. At any given moment, she would open her mouth and the angelic lyrics to Ripperton's "Loving You" would wrap around his heart. He knew he had to get used to living without it. Something he dreaded. It would not be easy, this much he knew.

"I've always—" she started, interrupted by a gut-wrenching cough.

Rubbing his chin, Julian cringed at the rough, staccato sound. "Are you okay? Some water?

Grace cleared her throat a couple times, which sounded more horrific. She nodded. "I'm fine. How are you this morning?" She cleared her throat again.

Turning to face the love of his life, Julian's smile was wide as a piercing blue ocean and as bright as the sun. Walking over to the bed, he stood motionless while maintaining the smile Grace loved so much, although forced.

"I should ask you the same thing. By the smile on your face while you were sleeping, you were cheating on me again." He held a stern look for a few seconds before releasing a hearty chuckle. "I hope it was as good for Chiwetel as it was for you."

She faintly laughed. "Yes, well…I love me a man in red kinky boots," she said, referencing *Kinky Boots*, which was the first time she saw Chiwetel Ejiofor on the big screen and fell madly in love with him, "but not as much as I love me some

Julian Winters. Yes, Lord. I sure do love me some of that handsome man with the big—"

"Stop it." He blushed. "I thought you would never wake up, Gracie. I'd be better if you weren't in here. How are you feeling, sweetheart?"

Grace tilted her head and turned up the corners of her mouth. "Hmm. Fair-to-middling, I suppose."

Julian gazed at her as if seeing her for the first time with her beautiful bald head and ashen complexion. He desired her flawless, almond hue once gain. He wanted to run his fingers through her once-flowing honey blonde ringlets. Julian missed how they used to dance about her now-pronounced forehead, thanks to her massive weight loss. Yet no matter how she looked, in his eyes, Grace was the most beautiful woman in the world. He loved the way she used to swipe a loose curl from her brow and tuck it behind her ear; it was so sexy to him. Now, she only swiped at a fly if it got close enough.

Julian reached for the chair positioned against the wood-grained double closet and pulled it over to her bedside. Sitting, he leaned forward, resting his upper torso on the edge of the bed. Clasping his hands, he smiled, puckered his delectable lips, and blew a soft kiss.

Palm stretched wide, she grasped at the air and clutched his kiss. Her strength was dissipating; holding an ink pen between her tiny fingers had become difficult. With shaky limbs, she brought his air kiss up to her lips, closed her eyes, and savored it. She cringed a bit from the pain that shot throughout her.

Noticing, he sat upright. "What's wrong, Gracie?"

She pursed her lips and gave two shakes of her head.

"Are you in pain, honey?"

"I'll be okay, Julian." Grace patted his hand. "Sweetie, how long have you been here?" Her voice was weak and faint, soft like cotton, just above a whisper. Recently, Julian strained to hear her, but he would strain for the rest of his life if it meant her living. It was selfish of him to think that way, he knew, but being selfish took priority. He wanted her to live.

Not confident in her reassurance, Julian clasped her hands in his and lowered his head before responding. "Not long… about an hour. You were sleeping so peacefully. I didn't want to wake you."

"I appreciate that, honey. Nurses been poking and prodding all night long. The only time I can rest is during the day."

"I've taken the day off, so you have me all to yourself."

"Wonderful! I've been missing you like crazy, too."

"Sweetness, *I'm* the one who is missing *you* like crazy." He shook his head, blinking several times, attempting to hold back forthcoming stinging tears. "The house isn't the same anymore. It feels strange without you there. It's too quiet." He wiped the rim of his eye, catching the tear before it fell, blinking back the others.

"Why don't you get a dog or a cat?"

"A what?"

"Or, maybe a parrot or some kind of bird to keep you company?"

Julian shook his head and smirked. "It truly amazes me how you can find humor in all of this."

"Well, you know my motto: It is what it is." She smiled, but knowing deep inside the only person she was lying to was herself. For the love of her life, her soul mate, Grace had to keep up the façade, and for him, she would do it.

"Babe, I—"

She squeezed his hand, cutting him off. "Honey, *please* don't do this to yourself. I love you so very much, Julian."

That did it. Why did she have to say that? The dam broke and tears streamed down his face. Torn up, he felt it difficult at times to control his emotions in front of her. It was something he never had to do. They shared everything, never withholding anything from each other. She knew her man inside out and he knew her. *There will never be another like her*, he surmised, as he cried like a baby.

"What am I supposed to do, Gracie, live life without you? I can't do that." In a tiny fit of anger, Julian jumped to his feet, kicking the chair, jabbing his fist in anger. "I just can't do that! I won't do it! I'll take my own life before I do that!" He ran his fingers through his curly tresses. "Damn it," he mumbled.

With his back to her, he was now pissed with himself. He tried so hard to be strong for her, not letting her see him break, but found it difficult to do. Right before his eyes, his woman was battling a fight she was certain to lose. Who in the fuck should have to experience this? He vowed to take care of her, but this feeling of helplessness was too much for

25

him to bear. Julian hugged himself and lowered his head. Oh, how he missed her hugs. She was too fragile to hug him now.

"Oh, Gracie, how can I manage without you, babe?" From deep within, he pulled out a cry that was silent, but felt deep in his heart. He was supposed to be the strong one, with her being so weak. The tables had turned. She was dying and strong, and he was living and powerless. He felt useless.

Grabbing hold of the bed railing, Grace tried to pull herself up in the bed, but she lacked the strength. She fell back onto the pillow. Admiring his weakness, Grace smiled and made a feeble attempt to calm him. "Listen, I know what you're going through. But," she sighed, "we have to accept reality for what it is."

"I just can't—"

"You have no choice. Everyone dies, Julian. Your time will come, too, and I will be waiting for you in Heaven, standing right next to God."

He walked toward the bed and plopped down into the chair. Julian slumped forward, laying all of his weight onto the bed, resting his head on her stomach.

"Why do you have to talk like that?" He pouted. "Ain't nobody thinking about God!"

"Julian!"

"Well…" He sat back in the chair, crossed one leg over the other, and twiddled his thumbs.

"If you keep talking like that, you will be standing at the gates of hell." She smirked. "Trust and believe you won't find me there." She chuckled lightly, cracking herself up.

His posture straightened like an arrow, with a tear-soaked face. "Grace!"

"What? I thought it was funny." She reached out for him. He leaned in. She stroked his face. "There, there, baby. Everything is going to be all right."

His mask of sadness was putting her into a bad headspace. It was becoming too much for Grace and she couldn't take any more of it.

"Honey, I don't mean to be rude or anything, but if you're going to keep crying every time you come here, then," she paused, looking away from him, "I'd rather you not come." There, she'd said it and it broke her heart.

Julian's eyes widened as his mouth gaped open.

Sweetheart," she continued, "listen to me." Grace looked into his hazel eyes, speckled with flecks pain. "I have come to terms with my fate. You should do the same. I love you. You are a wonderful, loving and devoted husband—given me more than I could ever dream of—and my heart is full, and…well, I'm tired, Julian." She looked around the room and out the window. "I'm tired of fighting a losing battle. I suppose I could reminisce about all the things I could have done differently, but what is the use?"

Julian focused in on her soft brown eyes—so serene, patient, and comforting—her eyes always calmed him during the most trying times.

With the back of her hand, Grace wiped the tears from his face.

27

"You're ready to leave me?"

"Of course not, but I'll always be with you." She stroked her frail fingers over his damp face. "You know, I have no regrets…except one."

"What's that?"

"I regret that I was never able to give you a son."

He smiled and shook his head. "Your unselfishness amazes me."

"Love is not selfish, Julian."

Julian rose from the chair, and walked over to the sink to splash water on his face.

"Are you thirsty?"

She stretched her arms above her head.

"Yes, but I am *dying* for a Pepsi." Grace cracked herself up as she fell out into a wicked giggle. "Get it, Julian, *dying*?"

Turning off the spigot, Julian snapped, "Don't say that!" He felt it wasn't funny, but he wished he had her strength, her endurance, and her ability to make light of something so devastating.

Grace smiled and felt it unnecessary to respond. She didn't know of any way she could ease his pain. Her death was inevitable, and this much he knew, but accepting it was the hardest thing he'd ever have to do. It was hard for her, too. However, she had accepted it and she hoped he would too. She realized it was asking too much of a man who loved his woman more than he loved himself, let alone anything or anyone else. She was ready to take her place at the foot of the throne, knowing it would end all her pain, but increase his. Julian would be fine, she was sure of it. Despite how he felt at that moment, God had him.

She reclined, resting her head on the pillow. She closed her eyes and hummed a tune she'd come to adore, "Take Me To The King," by Tamela Mann. "Truth is I'm tired," she sang, "options are few…" Hearing Tamela's voice in her head soothed and comforted her.

Feeling the dam water building, ready to explode, Julian knew that was his cue to leave the room. "I'll go to the cafeteria and get you a Pepsi."

"Thank you, sweetheart."

Julian smiled. "Anything else I can get for you?"

Grace shook her head and continued humming.

As Julian's hand wrapped around the door's handle, Grace opened her eyes and stared at his back.

He sensed her piercing glare. Tears started to flow once again, glistening down his face. *Shit! Shit! Shit!*

Seeing Julian in such pain was killing her more than the cancer, but she knew once she was gone, he'd be fine. Or would he?

"A bag of Doritos, please."

Julian nodded. "I'll be back."

"I'll be here." She reached for the handheld apparatus to administer a quick injection of morphine through her IV as deep pain racked her insides. "Fuck," she mumbled.

He quickly twirled around. "Gracie!"

29

"What? I can't cuss now?"

"Well, yeah…just you never do."

"Yeah, well, I feel like saying words I don't normally say, like goddamn it, kiss my ass, motherfucker, shit, shit, shit—"

Nodding, he smiled. "I get the picture. I'll be back."

Chapter 4

Julian walked by the hospital's gift shop, in route to the cafeteria. He came to an abrupt stop. A pink stuffed elephant caught his attention. Grace loved elephants, no matter the color, but she was a loyal member of Delta Sigma Theta, so a *pink* elephant wouldn't do.

She would kill me, he thought, chuckling as he imagined the look on her face if he walked into her room carrying a big-ass, pink elephant. His silent chuckle turned into a hearty laughter. It had been months since he had laughed and it felt good.

Entering the Gift Shop, Julian approached the counter and asked if the pink elephant was available in red.

"What you see is all that we have, sir." The elderly, white-haired volunteer clerk smiled widely. "The pink is beautiful, though."

"Yes, it is. I'll take it and a couple magazines, too, please."

"Which magazines would you like?"

Smiling, he said, "She loves Oprah's and *Essence*."

The clerk returned with the items. "Can I get you anything else, sir?"

Julian looked around and spotted the glass-encased refrigerator. "Oh yes, my wife is *dying* for a Pepsi." He smiled at his words, trying to do as Grace would want him to do, come to terms with the inevitable. He felt emotions rise in his throat, lodging at his Adam's apple again. He swallowed hard, rifling through his wallet.

"How much?"

The clerk looked at him. Her heart ached for him. Unfortunately, it wasn't anything new. She saw his kind before, day after day. *Poor thing*, she thought.

"Thirty-two dollars and fifteen cents."

Handing her a fifty-dollar-bill, Julian grabbed the elephant and white plastic bag with the Pepsi and magazines inside.

"Thank you. Keep the change."

"Thank you." She smiled, putting his change in the small jar beside the register labeled: Donate to the Children's Wing.

Leaving the Gift Shop, he walked toward the lobby and took a seat in the row of waiting room standard burgundy leather chairs facing the Patient Information desk. He buried his face in the plush, stuffed elephant and cried softly for a while. He needed that release. He needed to wallow in his own tears, if only for a few minutes, if only with a stuffed animal.

Julian opened the door to Doctor Lockett standing over Grace's bed, his fingers wrapped around her tiny, frail wrist, checking her pulse. Julian stood still, holding his breath, searching the doctor's face for anything indicating a change in his wife's condition. He refused to give up hope.

"Are you resting comfortably?" Doctor Lockett asked Grace.

"Yes," she sighed, "as much as I can."

"I know it's hard to rest when your vitals are being checked every hour." He chuckled.

Julian walked toward them. He placed the elephant at the foot of the bed.

"Wow, honey, they didn't have one in red?"

Julian smiled. "I asked, too. I guess you'll be an AKA for a while."

"Never!" she blurted, followed by a hearty laughter.

Julian turned toward Doctor Lockett. "So how is my queen, doctor?"

"She's doing just fine." He smiled.

The sullen look on Julian's face turned into a hardened frown. Doctor Lockett's response angered the hell out of him.

"No," he snapped, "she's not doing *just fine*. She's *dying*, doctor!" His anger spewed out between clenched teeth with poisonous venom. "How dare you make light of it?"

Grace called out to Julian a few times, but he could not hear her over his building fit of rage.

"My wife is dying!" He slammed the bottle of Pepsi down on the movable table at her bedside. "I wish you wouldn't act as though everything is so goddamn peachy keen!"

"Julian, please! It's not his fault."

Julian psychotically paced the floor with his hands stuffed inside his pockets "No? Then whose fault is it?" His arms flailed in the air.

"It's no one's fault, sweetheart. Please calm down. I can't take too much more of this."

"My wife is dying and there isn't a goddamn thing I can do about it! Do you know how that shit feels, doctor? Do you? I can't protect her and neither can you, goddamn it!"

"Julian, please stop taking the Lord's name in vain."

He rushed up to Doctor Lockett and stood his stance. "What fucking good are you, huh, Doc?"

Doctor Lockett understood Julian's anger all too well. "Mr. Winters," he hesitated.

Julian arrogantly folded his arms across his chest. "What? You're going to tell me that you know how *I* feel?" His voice oozed sarcasm. He chuckled. "Yeah, that's what they all do."

Grace's calm demeanor subsiding, the blush in her cheeks showed her dismay. "Julian, damn it! All of this is working my fucking nerves. I'm dying and the *last* damn thing I want are people around me arguing over the inevitable. So please, do me this one favor... shut the fuck up or get the hell out!"

Julian faced her in disbelief. The woman who had been so meek, timid, and sweet throughout their marriage was telling him to shut the fuck up or get the hell out. A smile graced his lips. Her outburst eased his anger. He looked at Doctor Lockett. "My apologies, Doctor."

"It's no problem, really. Actually, I do know how you feel, Mr. Winters. I lost my wife to ovarian cancer. I am a doctor and couldn't save my own wife. I was helpless and weak. She was the strong one," he faced Grace, "much like your wife."

"Most women are," Grace mumbled, tucking the sheet up under her chin.

Julian lowered his head. He felt like a complete fool, as if he was the only man in the world experiencing such intolerable, gut-wrenching pain.

Doctor Lockett caressed Julian's shoulder, as a show of comradery. "Well, I need to get back to my other patients. Mrs. Winters, please don't hesitate to let the nurses or me know if you need anything...anything at all."

Grace was quite upset, but her smile remained warm and comforting. "Thank you. I'll keep that in mind."

She waited for Doctor Lockett to leave the room before directing an annoyed look in her husband's direction.

"I'm sorry, Gracie. Don't be mad at me."

Her face softened, as she understood, unable to imagine what she would do if the shoe were on the other foot. "Yeah, yeah." She smiled. "Where is my Pepsi?"

She reached for the bottle of Pepsi and, with much effort, unscrewed the top. She tilted her head back, closed her eyes, and grazed her lips with the mouth of the bottle, feeling the coolness against her dry, chapped lips. Grace parted her lips and allowed the ice-cold beverage to seep between them, swooshing the liquid around in her mouth before allowing it to flow down her throat. She slowly gulped, feeling the cold, carbonated, refreshing liquid flow deep inside her chest and into her shrinking stomach, before swiping the back of her hand across her pale, thin-pursed lips. "That was so good," she said, between a couple good hearty belches.

Julian laughed and sat on the foot of the bed.

Grace sat the bottle on the movable bed table and pushed it to the side with as much strength as she could muster.

"Honey," she whispered.

Julian looked up and into her eyes. "Yes."

"Where are my Doritos?"

"Oh, sorry, Gracie, I forgot."

She shrugged. "Hey, while you were gone, I was thinking about the first time we met. Do you remember?"

"Yes, I remember." He caressed her blanket-covered knee. "I thought you were sent by God, and I still do."

"You always did know the right things to say. You're such the Casanova."

"That happens when you're speaking the truth, Gracie."

She smiled.

Chapter 5

Sixteen years earlier…

Twenty-six-year-old Grace stood at the counter and sipped a cup of piping hot coffee. Long piano player's fingers wrapped around the twelve-ounce paper cup as the piping hot drink trickled down her throat, warming her insides on a cold January afternoon, with the current issue of *The Afro American Newspaper* tucked firmly under her arm. After paying for the coffee, she sought an empty table in the busy, local coffee shop.

Oblivious to all, she sat her purse and newspaper on the table before dropping the briefcase to the floor. Sitting, Grace crossed one long, stocking-covered curvaceous leg over the other and lightly feathered a loose, tendril from her brow. She pulled her laptop from the briefcase, flipped it open, and turned it on. Patiently waiting for it to warm up, as she sipped the hot Java and eyed the small coffee shop swarming with caffeine addicts, her eyes froze on the tall figure whose massive shoulders filled out the brown leather bomber jacket.

Standing tall, straight, and towering over everyone around him, he stuck out like a sore thumb. His large hands made the coffee cup disappear.

You know what they say about men with huge hands, she thought.

Feeling awkward staring at him, but unable to redirect her stare, her eyes wandered below his waist. His worn denim hugged his ass and caressed his bulge. *Damn!* The twitching between her thighs made her smile and think dirty thoughts about a stranger.

When he turned in her direction, their eyes met. His smile was warm and inviting, causing a twitching encore in her panties.

Embarrassed, Grace looked down at her laptop and closed her eyes. *What an idiot*, she thought, *might as well hang a sign on my forehead that reads* DESPERATE.

A slight smile curled the corner of his mouth, forming the cutest smirk. *She's a cutie*, he thought, as he swaggered toward her. His towering frame startled her.

Grace looked up from her laptop and nearly melted.

"Hello." He smiled, showcasing beautiful white teeth and deep, cave-like dimples.

Have mercy! She stammered over her thoughts, trying to find something to say that did not make her sound crazy.

"Usually when someone says hello to you, the courteous thing to do is respond in kind." He chuckled.

"I'm sorry, you're right. You caught me off guard." She smiled sheepishly. "Hello."

"I noticed you were seated alone. Will someone be joining you?"

Grace shook her head.

He motioned toward the chair. "Do you mind?"

"No."

"Thank you. I'm Julian, and you are?"

"Grace. Nice to meet you, Julian."

"Nice to meet you, too, Gracie. You're stunning." He gazed at her.

"*Grace*. My name is Grace."

"Yes, that's what I said."

"No, you called me *Gracie*. My name is Grace."

"Oh, I see…Grace. My apologies." Julian admired her beautiful tresses and smooth, almond complexion. He wasn't sure of her ethnicity, but he didn't care. At first glance, he knew she would be his. "You know, Gracie, I believe in being forthright, this way there will be no confusion and if you choose you want to roll with it, then cool."

"I beg your pardon!"

"I find you sexy. I want to make love to you."

Grace broke out into hysterical laughter. "Are you kidding me?"

"No, I'm not. In fact, I want to marry you…someday."

Her laughter shifted to a blank stare. "Really?"

"I know what you're thinking."

"Do you now?"

"Yes. You're thinking I'm full of shit."

"Bingo!"

"I do want to make love to you…after we're married, of course."

Julian was handsome, for sure, and no man had ever approached her in such a manner. That smile, shining brighter than a full moon, warmed her insides. Grace was feeling a little frisky and wondered what would happen if she acted upon it. It had been a while since her last oil change and she was feeling a little dry. She'd run down her last two AA batteries, so her silver bullet was out of commission until she made it to Rite Aid.

She leaned back in her seat, folded her arms over her chest, and pouted. "So, let me see if I understand what you're proposing. You don't know me from a bowl of grits, you don't want to call me by my given name, and you want to have sex with me?"

"No, I don't want to have sex with you. I want to make love to you, but after we're married, and I like Gracie."

40

Unfolding her arms, Grace placed her palms on the table. She sipped her now warm coffee. "There's no difference between the two, and I don't know about that marriage thing. Gracie sounds old."

"Oh, there's a difference between having sex and making love. Yes, you will marry me…in due time, and it doesn't sound old. It sounds sweet, just like you are."

"Yes, except you don't love me. So, it would be sex and I don't marry dudes I don't know."

"I don't need to know you to make love to you. I know your spirit. Besides, using the phrase, 'having sex' is so impersonal. Don't you think? Especially for your future husband."

There were touches of humor around his mouth and near his eyes that intrigued her. She was actually contemplating his proposal. What in the hell was she thinking?

"So, uh…what do I get in return?" Grace asked, knowing how stupid the question sounded.

"What you'll get in return is a man who will adore your life and the best love you've ever had." Julian leaned in closer. "The kind that will have your sweet pussy throbbing for this big dick for days; the kind you will want over and over; the kind you will marry for because you'll want it all the time; the kind—"

Grace turned her head to the side to avert his gaze, but the sudden rosiness of her cheeks gave her away. "Okay, I get the point. I don't think I want to play this game anymore." She gathered her things.

"Sure you do."

Grace stood up, pushing the back of the chair with her strong legs. "No, I don't. Now, if you'll excuse me." She grabbed her belongings and headed out the establishment and toward her vehicle.

Julian was quickly on her heels. "Is this how it will always be, Gracie?"

Her heart raced rapidly, not from fear, but from the anticipation of giving in to him. She wanted to be with him, but it was silly and he was a stranger after all. *He could be some kind of axe murderer or something*, she pondered.

"My name is Grace!"

"Wait, Gracie, please."

"Grace!" She threw up her hand. "My damn name is Grace!"

Digging in her purse, she grabbed out her keys and dropped them on the ground. Julian quickly picked them up and placed them gently in her hand, not releasing it.

"I'm sorry…Grace. Please, can we start over?"

In deep consideration, Grace snatched her hand from his, unlocked the car door, opened it, and tossed her things in the back seat.

"I'm sorry, Gracie," he cleared his throat, "Grace." He smiled.

"I don't know what kind of women you're used to, but you have me twisted—"

"I know, and I'm sorry. It was stupid of me to approach you the way I did."

"I would prefer dinner, conversation, a few dates, an AIDS test, and anything else I can think of before you try taking me to bed!"

Regret washed over him like waves on a shallow beach. Julian took a step backward. He was out of line, had taken the wrong approach. "I'm really sorry. I'll let you be. I was," he paused, gazing into her beautiful eyes, "being an idiot. That's what I get for listening to my friends."

When Julian turned to walk away, Grace opened her mouth to speak. Then, her mouth closed and she got into her car. Whom was she fooling? Surely not herself as she was interested, but he was coming on a little too strong for her taste. While his approach was enticing, it also scared the mess out of her.

She sighed heavily and rolled down the car window.

"Hey, Julian! Have you ever heard of foreplay?"

"Yes, I love their music." He smiled.

Grace chuckled. Her apprehension abated somewhat under the warm glow of his smile. The beginning of a smile tipped the corners of her mouth.

"You have a beautiful smile," he said, moving toward her car. Upon approach, he bent down and looked her in the eyes. "Can we start over?"

"I would like that."

Julian trotted around to the passenger side of her car.

She looked at him strangely, but unlocked the door for him.

"Let's go to my place," he suggested.

"Now see!"

"Just joking."

43

"I do know of a place where we can go and talk, if you'd like," she offered. I would be much more comfortable there."

"Sounds good to me."

Grace looked at him, puzzled.

"Yes?"

"Where's your car?" she asked him, her brows arched. "I do not drive men around."

"Ah, yes. I'm parked over there." He pointed his long finger in the direction of his car. "It is the black Range Rover. See it?"

"Yes, I see it. Why don't you get in your black Range Rover and follow me?"

"Anything for you, beautiful." Julian rushed out of her car and jogged to his vehicle.

Grace started the engine and drove to the only place she felt comfortable—her condominium.

What was she thinking, bringing a complete stranger to her home? "Would you like some coffee?"

"Not unless we're planning to be up all night." He chuckled.

"Well, I don't have any alcohol. I don't drink the hard stuff. But there may be a bottle of wine in the fridge."

"That's cool, I don't need any." Julian followed Grace into the living room, watching the delightful sway in her rear end. He shook his head with delight. He was going to enjoy caressing that ass.

"Get comfortable," she said, "while I get out of these shoes. My feet are killing me."

Julian stood in the middle of the floor and watched her as she disappeared into the bedroom. He took off his jacket and started to lay it across the sofa, but quickly changed his mind and draped it over his arm instead. The sofa was white as snow like the other furniture in her home. Her place looked more like a showplace than a place to relax. The only splash of color was a huge, beautiful art piece by Charles Bibbs hanging over the sofa. He was really digging her taste, but it did not feel too homey to him.

"I'll be out in a minute," she yelled from the back. "Help yourself to whatever is in the fridge."

"Thanks." He draped his jacket over the back of the white dining room chair, but by this time, he did not care. *Can't imagine having furniture I can't sit on*, he thought, slithering into the kitchen. Julian peeked into the refrigerator. He reached inside and pulled out a bottle of wine unknown to him: JazzBerry by Boordy Vineyards. He thought the bottle was interesting because of its unique label. His first time seeing a wine bottle with people partying on the label, he shrugged. Searching the kitchen cabinets, Julian located two wine goblets, and headed for the dining room, sitting the glasses on the glass-topped table supported by two lion statues. He admired it; something he never thought to do, but interesting nonetheless. He popped the cork and partially filled the glasses.

"You have a nice place," he shouted, wondering why it was taking her so long to change her shoes. "Are you going to be much longer?" Now Julian was becoming concerned. *Maybe this wasn't a good idea after all. She could be a stalker or worse… Lizzy Borden, maybe.* He chuckled.

After a fifteen-minute wait, she finally graced him with her presence. "That wasn't too long, was it?"

"I thought I was going to have to call in the National Guard." He laughed.

"Yes, well, I had to get myself…uh, in the mood. I've never brought a stranger home before."

"I can dig it, but I'm sure you'll have no regrets."

Grace nodded toward the glasses sitting on the table. "I see you found the wine."

"Yes, I hope you don't mind. I thought we both could use a glass…to unwind."

She reached for her wine before he could do the honors. With the glass pressed against her lips, she flung her head back as the red liquid vanished down her throat. He looked at her in astonishment. Grace extended the glass toward him.

As he began to pour, she said, "To the rim, please."

Julian's eyes left the glass and darted to her. *Not a damn lush*, he wondered. He cared less for an alcoholic.

After two more, full-to-the-rim glasses of wine, Grace inhaled and exhaled with a long sigh. "Well, are you ready?"

"Ready for what?"

"To love me."

Julian glared into her eyes. They were quite glossy, reminiscent of a drunkard.

"I thought you weren't—"

"Don't kill the mood," she said, pressing her finger against his lips.

He nodded. "Okay, well, how about a little music?"

"Sure, what's your pleasure?"

"Something soft."

Grace moved toward the iPod sitting on the end table, turned it on, and scrolled through the selection of song titles.

"I can give you diamonds," Alicia Keys belted out.

"I really love this song," she said. "Hell, I love all of her songs."

"The sister is very talented and attractive to boot."

Her eyes roamed the room; she was feeling uneasy.

Julian took a step closer, grabbed her hands, and caressed them. He pulled her into him. His lips brushed against hers. The hairs on the back of her neck stood as she tensed.

"Relax, Gracie." He wrapped his arms around her.

The tense lines on her face disappeared, her body relaxing in his arms. She liked that name after all.

He kissed her earlobe. She slightly moaned. Kissing her cheek, he slid his hand under her blouse and cupped her breast. Her body stiffened from his touch as the throb between her thighs intensified. She flinched at every caress and pinch of her areola.

Grace was unable to control the spasmodic trembling within her. With a swift motion, her blouse eased over her head and billowed to the floor. Julian removed her bra and knelt down before her. He unzipped her skirt and it fell down around her red-painted, manicured toes. He tongue-stroked her nipples, then trailed down to her moistened cove, and lightly blew. A delightful shiver coursed through her. He slithered his snakelike tongue through her opening and tasted her essence. She felt the blood surge from the top of her head to the tips of her toes. Her body heaved, her breasts jutting upward as his finger slithered through her juices, finding the spot. She raised her arms above her head and stretched. She softly cooed. His shaft stiffened.

"That feels so good, Julian." Grace moved her hips in a slow, circular motion, followed by a deep-throated moan.

Julian looked up at her. "Come down here."

She lowered down next to him and watched him unbuckle his belt. As his fingers moved toward the button of his jeans, she stopped him.

"Let me," Grace offered, smiling. "Lay back."

As he sat on the floor and reclined against the white sofa, she leaned into his abdomen and puckered her gloss-stained lips. Grace inhaled deeply as she unbuttoned his jeans and unzipped the zipper. Julian smelled refreshing. Searching down his pants, she found his hardened shaft and pulled it out in the open. With her mouth closed, she gasped. His penis was beautiful, thick, smooth, and even-toned.

As she kissed the head of his love, Julian placed his hand on the back of her head. His head fell backward. His heart jolted and his pulse pounded as she took him into the back of her throat, fellating him.

"*Damn*, woman," he moaned.

He pulled her on top of him.

"Wait one second," she whispered. "I'll be right back."

Grace darted for the bedroom and returned with a condom. Using her teeth, she tore open the silver package and pulled out the latex sheath, tossing the wrapper to the side. She placed it on the tip of the head and rolled it down his hardened steel. Grace leaned down and kissed him as she straddled him, lowering down on him. His hands slowly moved downward, skimming both sides of her body to her thighs, down to the opening of her vaginal lips, searching for her pleasure points. He flicked her swollen bud with his finger until they both climaxed.

Reveling in exhaustive bliss, Grace lay beside Julian as he leaned over and, with his tongue, stroked her hardened nipple, down to the opening of her garden. Without thought, she spread her thighs. He nestled his face in her cave, drowning in her juices until she climaxed again.

He looked up at her, gazing into her eyes. "You're going to be my wife."

Chapter 6

Current Day

Julian slightly chuckled and moved up on the bed, leaning in to kiss her lips. "I love you," he cooed, rubbing his warm nose against her cold one. The warm breath oozing from his slightly parted lips warmed her insides.

She shivered.

"You cold?"

"A little. My temperature is dropping." She spoke without an ounce of concern.

"Stop it, Grace."

"I'm sorry."

"It's okay."

Feeling the strength slowly drain from her, Grace managed to whisper, "Love me one last time."

Closing his eyes tightly, he shook his head and poked out his bottom lip. "Baby, I want nothing more than to love you.

If loving you is going to keep you here with me, then I will love you with all my might, and as hard as I can, but..."

Julian stood up. Gently, he pulled back the covers and admired her fading beauty as he lifted her hospital gown up over her stomach, exposing her soft genitals that looked as right as rain to him.

She lowered the gown and turned her head to the side.

"What's wrong, Gracie?"

"I'm ugly."

"No you're not, babe." He leaned down and passionately kissed her lips. Then he pulled back and stared into her beautiful brown eyes. "You are the most beautiful woman in the world."

Once again, Julian raised her gown above her stomach and caressed her thighs, softly touching and caressing, moving upward and over her frailness as he rose to the occasion. He wanted so badly to love her and mesh with her one last time. He wanted her scent stitched in his body for a lifetime. He would give his soul to feel her being, storing it in his memory for years to come. Yet, she was too frail and he would probably do her more harm.

"Oh, Julian, you've always known how to make me feel good," she cooed, with closed lids and a satisfied smile on her face, her lips turned up into the sexiest smirk that was truly Grace Winters. "I would give anything to feel you one last time."

"Sweet, sweet, baby," he whispered, brushing his lips against hers. "I want so badly to be inside you, but I don't think it's a good idea, babe."

"Why not?" Grace's voice cracked, a soft cry welling in her throat. "You don't want me anymore, Julian? I know I'm not—"

He shushed her. "Woman, don't be silly. I'm about to bust. I want to be inside of you so badly. But—"

"But, what?"

"But, I don't want to hurt you."

"You could never hurt me, Julian. Please, make love to me one last time. I'm begging you."

"You never have to beg me for anything, sweetheart."

With his hands propped on his hips, he contemplated the possible consequences of his pending action. Julian realized he would hurt her more by denying her. Unbuckling his belt, he unzipped his pants and allowed them to fall to the floor.

Grace giggled.

"What's funny?"

"Suppose a nurse comes in and catches us."

"It will be much more exciting. Shall we call one in so we can get this party started?"

Grace laughed aloud. "You have no sense at all." She smacked him on the arm. "Now mount your filly and get to riding, *Big Daddy*."

"Now you know that turns me on!"

Julian rushed toward the door.

"Where are you going?"

"One minute." He propped a chair under the door handle and looked at Grace. "Do you think that will work?"

She nodded with a chuckle.

"What's so funny?"

Like a blushing schoolgirl, she pointed at his erection. "You're good and ready for me!"

Smirking, he grabbed his erection and walked toward her bed.

Peering into her eyes, his heart melted. As he gently climbed on top of her, she parted her thighs. His love muscle aimed for her sweet target, steadily he guided it, head first, into her beautiful, sweet abyss, careful not to put too much weight on her or get too excited. He shivered as he slipped inside her; it felt amazing.

A soft moan escaped her.

He stopped. "Am I hurting you?"

She shook her head. "I love you so much, Julian."

Careful not to rest all of him on on her, he closed his eyes and cried internally, as he loved his woman one last time.

The following morning, Grace woke to Julian sleeping in the chair under the window. Smiling, she reminisced about the previous night. Every kiss sewn on her body was a stitch into her soul. She would take it with her into eternity.

Feeling chilly, she pulled the crisp white blanket under her chin and silently cried. She said a silent prayer, too.

"Dear God," she paused, blinking several times before she thought of the next words that followed. "Thank you for loving me all these years." She looked over at Julian. "I am sure you know how Julian's feeling. He's angry, God, but please forgive him and help him to cope and live through all this. It hasn't been easy for him and it's only going to get worse." The captive tear that escaped down her cheek absorbed into the blanket. Grace took in a deep breath, pursed her lips, and slowly exhaled. "I know that in Your mansion, there are many rooms, God, and I'm hoping you've prepared one for me. I promise I will be the perfect houseguest." She smiled and looked upward. "I'm really looking forward to seeing you, God. If you don't mind, could you have my mama and daddy with you when I come home? I would really appreciate it. In the name of your son, Jesus, Amen."

The morning shift nurse entered the room, interrupting Grace's private moment with God. "Good Morning, Mrs. Winters. How are we feeling this morning?"

"We are feeling fine, thank you."

"That's good." The nurse placed her breakfast tray on the table. Looking over at Julian, she asked, "Can I get him a blanket?"

"That would be nice of you, thank you."

Retrieving the hospital-regulated blanket from the top of the double closet, the nurse placed it over a peacefully sleeping Julian.

"He's so exhausted, I'm sure," said Grace. "I can't seem to get him to go home."

"He doesn't want to leave your side. No one can blame him for that," the nurse replied, standing at the bedside. "Okay, so is there anything I can get for you, Mrs. Winters?"

"Yes, if you don't mind, could you please get me a Bible?"

The nurse turned up her lips and smiled. She'd never received such a request. "Sure, I'll see what I can do."

Grace smiled and nodded. "Thank you. I'd like to do a little meditating before He sends for me, which will be soon. So, if you could make it quick, I'd really appreciate it. I don't have much time."

With a smile and a nod, the nurse exited the room on the hunt for a Bible.

Peeking over at Julian, who was still fast asleep, she mustered all the strength she could and pulled herself up in the bed. After a brief pause, to catch her breath, she swung her legs over the edge of the bed and scooted her bottom to the edge.

Hearing her move about, Julian woke and sat upright in the chair.

"Gracie! What are you doing?"

"Oh, nothing, I'll be fine."

"Sweetie, let me help you."

"I'm okay, Julian."

Julian jumped to his feet, knocking the blanket to the floor and rushed over to her side. "I'll help you. What is it you needed?"

"I want to get down on my knees."

"Why do you want to kneel on this cold floor, Gracie?"

Annoyed, she jerked away from his grasp. "If you're not going to help me, then go sit down!"

"All right, calm down. Here," he retrieved the pillow from her bed and dropped it to the floor, "use the pillow."

On her knees, Grace leaned against the edge of the bed and clasped her hands. She closed her eyes.

"Pray with me, please, Julian."

Every emotion in his body forced its way from the pit of his stomach up to his throat. Julian couldn't speak. He felt like throwing up as a tight knot formed in his belly. He, too, got on his knees, clasped his hands, and closed his eyes.

"Our Father, who art in heaven," Grace softly prayed. "Hallowed be thy name. Thy Kingdom come."

Julian cleared his throat and prayed with his wife. "Thy will be done, on earth as it is in heaven."

She coughed, followed by a heavy sigh.

"You okay, Gracie?"

She nodded.

"Give us this day our daily bread," they continued together. "And forgive us our trespasses as we forgive those who trespass against us. And, lead us not into temptation, but deliver us from evil. For thine is the kingdom, and the power, and the glory, forever. Amen."

Folding her arms before her, Grace lowered her head and rested in peace. God answered her prayers. God had forgiven her and called her home to bask in one of the many rooms that He prepared for her.

Opening his eyes, Julian wiped away the storm of tears and looked over at his beloved Grace.

"Gracie," he called out to her. "Baby…" He gently touched her shoulder.

Realizing she was gone, he wrapped his arms around her and lifted her, cradling her in his arms, savoring their final embrace, and laid her on the bed. Julian climbed into bed with her and held her close. The floodgate of emotions opened as he said goodbye to his soul mate, the love of his life, and best friend.

"I love you, Grace. I'll see you soon."

Chapter 7

An hour after grievers departed, Julian stood over the opened grave. The earth smelled damp after yestereve's rain. All around him, tightly squeezed graves marked by plaques on the ground, the dead muttered in their hollows. His inner fight with God made him oblivious to it all.

Trimmed in gold, the white casket already lowered into the earth, her final resting place. What was he going to do without her? How would he go on? What on earth did he ever do to deserve such pain and rejection by God?

Julian looked around and up to the sky. He closed his eyes and pursed his lips tightly before he yelled, "Damn you!"

He dropped to his knees. The once gentle husband had turned into a bitter man. He buried his face in his hands and wept. The cries from deep within his belly were heart wrenching and like nothing he'd heard coming from himself. He never experienced such a pain, nor could he describe it.

Julian reached out for her, praying this was all a bad dream, but this was his reality. She was gone, only to return in his dreams.

"Gracie!" He grabbed the top of his head, his chin buried into his chest. "Gracie," he whimpered.

Julian sat back on the heels of his shoes, wiped his face, and inhaled deeply.

"I know you are in a better place, Gracie. I know you aren't in any more pain. I know you are at peace. But forgive me for being so selfish and wanting you here with me."

His angel was in heaven now and he could do nothing about it. Pulling himself up to stand and looked into the opened hole for the last time, Julian remembered their last intimate moment that will be forever etched in his mind. He straightened his posture and sighed heavily, remembering Grace's favorite lyrics from Minnie Ripperton's "Lovin' You." *'Cause lovin' you has made my life so beautiful.*

"You made loving you so easy, and I will never stop loving my Gracie."

Julian turned on his heels and walked toward his new life without the love of his life…without Grace…remembering when he loved her for the last time.

PREVIEW

Trespass

A Novel
Coming 2019

Furrowing arched eyebrows, she held her breath in protest against the stench that was knotting her stomach into a tight ball. An emotionally drained Kennedy Montgomery leaned against the seafoam-colored wall, riddled with scrapes and dents, left behind by gurneys and wheelchairs with years of stories to tell. The back of her head slightly touched the picture hanging overhead that matched the others of colorful landscapes lining the corridor. Next to her were double doors; an overhead red neon sign directed staff moving hurriedly across the black and white speckled tile flooring toward the restricted area that held the love of her life. Virginia Union Hospital was for the sick and people who needed healing, and right now, her heart was broken, her spirit was shattered, and her soul bled. Then, the reason why she occupied that lone space hit her and she gasped, panting in terror. Just thinking of it horrified her. She looked toward the doubled doors. What was going on back there? She felt inclined to barge through those doors for answers, but she knew better.

She hated hospitals, where sickness lingered and death lurked. Being there reminded her of the day her mother died. She would never forget that moment or feeling for as long as she lived. It was the day death snatched her heart from her chest; the day she wanted to end her own life. The day she crawled in bed with her beloved mother, saying her final goodbye. She never thought she would ever have that feeling again, until now. She felt ill. She wanted to faint. If anything happened to her, she would never forgive herself.

Kennedy hunched over, with her chin buried into her chest, gripping her knees, as tears threatened to escape for the thousandth time in the past few weeks. It seemed like crying had become her full-time occupation. She took deep breaths, attempting to steady her rapidly beating heart, its loud thumping echoing in her ears, driving her toward the edge of insanity. Thump. Thump. Thump. She took in slow, deep breaths, attempting to slow the quick-paced rhythm, but to no avail. She was a nervous, emotional mess. The extinguished overhead lights, which would have thrown light downward to illuminate her path, kept her in darkness, except for a faint spotlight off in the distance—appearing eerie, yet surprisingly calm. She checked her gold wristwatch. It was four o'clock in the morning, three hours after receiving the call.

Kennedy knew nothing of what was going on. One minute she was in Emporia, Virginia, and the next, she was speeding up Route 58 East, with a lump in her throat, a cigarette dangling from her trembling lips, tears blurring her vision, while holding a full-blown conversation with God. That phone call was a broken record in her mind, on a constant skip.

"Mrs. Montgomery?"

"Yes."

"Ma'am, this is Doctor Wesley from Virginia Union Hospital. We have your daughter, Lindsay, in our care—"

Inhaling deeply, she covered her mouth. *"What?"* Her body froze. A tear pushed through, balancing on the rim of her eyelid. One blink pushed it over the edge and down her cheek. Her loud, deep gasp interrupted him. Her heart dropped to her feet. She swiped away the falling tear.

"Your daughter was in a car accident. It was pretty bad. She's going to need surgery, and we need your permission to—"

"Oh, my God! Jesus, no!" She swallowed hard. *"Is my baby going to…going to…is she—"*

"No, ma'am, not if I can help it."

Closing her eyes, she reached for the pack of Newport cigarettes on the nightstand. *"Why does she need surgery?"*

"Your daughter is bleeding internally and I need to get inside of her to see what's going on."

"Oh, Jesus," she whispered, lighting the cigarette that dangled between her lips. She took what seemed like the longest drag in history.

"Ma'am?"

She exhaled a long stream of smoke. *"Yes. Yes, by all means, doctor. Please, do whatever you have to do to save my baby's life."*

Kennedy's life had turned upside down, spiraling into a dark abyss, and now this. She did not know how much more she could take. The stinging in her throat and burning sensation in her nose coaxed her tears to betray her, breaking through her tough exterior like crashing waves against a shore. Damn it, betrayal had taken up full-time residency in her heart, hanging up the NO VACANCY sign.

Exhausted, she stood upright, propping her hands on her hips, tilting her head back, staring up at the ceiling. Propping her Michael Kors' Claire lizard-embossed leather pumps against the wall, she glared across the hall into the waiting area to see if her matching purse was still laying in the burgundy leather chair where she left it. She wanted a cigarette; it was the only thing that had not betrayed her. It was reliable, but there was no smoking in the hospital and she refused to budge from that spot. Temptation was getting the best of her, until she was about to step forward. An overwhelming, familiar sensation gripped her like a thief in the night, stealing her breath. She jolted; a chill ran up her spine, causing a slight shiver.

At the far end of the hallway, under an overhead light, there he stood dressed in a fitted black V-neck shirt, tucked inside beige trousers, with a gold buckled black leather belt completing the ensemble. His rich, black, naturally curly hair, with flecks of silver gracing his temples, accentuated strong, arched brows, thick eyelashes, and deep, brown piercing eyes.

Distinct cheekbones, an angular jaw, and smooth mocha complexion made him exquisite. On any other day, her heart would melt at the sight of him. Now, her heart was hardened toward him.

Reginald Montgomery sensed the presence of his woman the moment he turned the corner. Kennedy was still as beautiful as the last time he saw her. His heart raced. She took his breath away. A slight smile graced his smooth, full lips as he recognized the blush pink blouse she wore. He had given it to her last Christmas. She wore her favorite jeans, too. Not too tight, hugging all the right curves. Her warm, brown hair color and fair skin made her full pink-stained lips stand out. He would give anything to kiss them again. He missed her like crazy. He longed for her. He craved to make love to her, to feel her strong legs wrapped around his waist, her arms around his neck, as they would gaze into each other's eyes. He prayed for the opportunity to make it up to her, to make things right. Could this be the time? Would she give him the time of day right now? He fucked up, this much he knew, but he also knew his wife. With time, he hoped, she would come around. He would give her the space she needed. He was not giving up on his marriage, on his family.

Staring at her, Reggie was frozen in place. Everything in him wanted to run to her, take her in his arms, hold her, kiss her, tell her how sorry he was, and that he would never do it again. He wanted to make things right between them, but he was no fool. She hated him, which he determined from the many unanswered phone calls and text messages. Yet, he could not take his eyes off her. Although it felt like hours of him staring at her, it had only been a few moments before his cell phone rang, jarring him from his stare, catching her attention.

She recognized it. That ringtone. Earth Wind & Fire's "That's The Way Of the World." Kennedy's form shifted, turning in his direction. Even though he appeared to be miles away, she knew her husband anywhere, and could pick him out of a lineup blindfolded. Damn, she missed him. She desired him. She wanted to run to him, wrap her arms around his neck, and devour his mouth, taste his sweet saliva, and inhale the scent of Dior's Sauvage. She needed to feel his arms around her, his strong hands palming her ass. His heat grinding inside her, loving her. She needed it, she need him. Hell, whom was she kidding? She loved him, it was true, but she could no longer think with her heart. She had to think with her head. She had to do what was best for her. She now had to be the guardian of her heart, since he abandoned his post.

Their eyes locked, their gaze intense. Slowly he moved his hand, wanting to reach out to her and move toward her, but the constant ringing cell phone stopped him. He broke their gaze and looked down at his phone. *Damn*, he thought.

With his head hung low, he raised his eyes upward.

She was gone.

Darting across the hall into the waiting room, Kennedy huddled in a darkened corner, praying the footsteps she heard weren't his. The steps moved frantically toward her. She closed her eyes and held her breath. *Please, God, not now. I just can't.*

ABOUT THE AUTHOR

JESSICA TILLES is an award-winning, national best-selling author of several books and an award-winning independent publisher. She has ghostwritten several books through the Literary Ghostwriter and founded TWA Solutions & Services (formerly The Writer's Assistant) to help authors accomplish their dreams of publishing their books, as well as providing other services.

CONNECT WITH JESSICA:
Her website: www.jessicatilles.com
TWA Solutions: www.twasolutions.com
Literary Ghostwriter: www.literaryghostwriter.com
Xpress Yourself Publishing: www.xpressyourselfpublishing.com
Social Media: @JessicaTilles
Facebook Fan page: @JessicaTillesAuthor